Dear Parents,

Welcome to the Scholastic Reader series. We have taken over 80 years of experience with teachers, parents, and children and put it into a program that is designed to match your child's interests and skills.

Level 1—Short sentences and stories made up of words kids can sound out using their phonics skills and words that are important to remember.

Level 2—Longer sentences and stories with words kids need to know and new "big" words that they will want to know.

Level 3—From sentences to paragraphs to longer stories, these books have large "chunks" of texts and are made up of a rich vocabulary.

Level 4—First chapter books with more words and fewer pictures.

It is important that children learn to read well enough to succeed in school and beyond. Here are ideas for reading this book with your child:

- Look at the book together. Encourage your child to read the title and make a prediction about the story.
- Read the book together. Encourage your child to sound out words when appropriate. When your child struggles, you can help by providing the word.
- Encourage your child to retell the story. This is a great way to check for comprehension.
- Have your child take the fluency test on the last page to check progress.

Scholastic Readers are designed to support your child's efforts to learn how to read at every age and every stage. Enjoy helping your child learn to read and love to read.

> **—Francie Alexander**
> Chief Education Officer
> Scholastic Education

For Kaia
R.I.

For Daisy and Owen
K.M.

Text copyright © 2003 by Rose Impey.
Illustrations copyright © 2003 by Katharine McEwen.
Originally published in the UK in 2003 under the title *Titchy Witch and the Frog Fiasco* by Orchard Books UK.

Published by Scholastic Inc.
SCHOLASTIC, CARTWHEEL BOOKS, and associated logos are trademarks and/or registered trademarks of Scholastic Inc.

Library of Congress Cataloging-in-Publication Data Available
ISBN 0-439-78451-4   11/07   3654   5894

10 9 8 7 6 5 4 3 2 1   06 07 08 09 10

Printed in the U.S.A.
First Scholastic printing, August 2006

Wanda Witch
and Too Many Frogs

Rose Impey ★ Katharine McEwen

Scholastic Reader — Level 3

Cartwheel
·B·O·O·K·S·®

SCHOLASTIC INC.

New York Toronto London Auckland Sydney
Mexico City New Delhi Hong Kong Buenos Aires

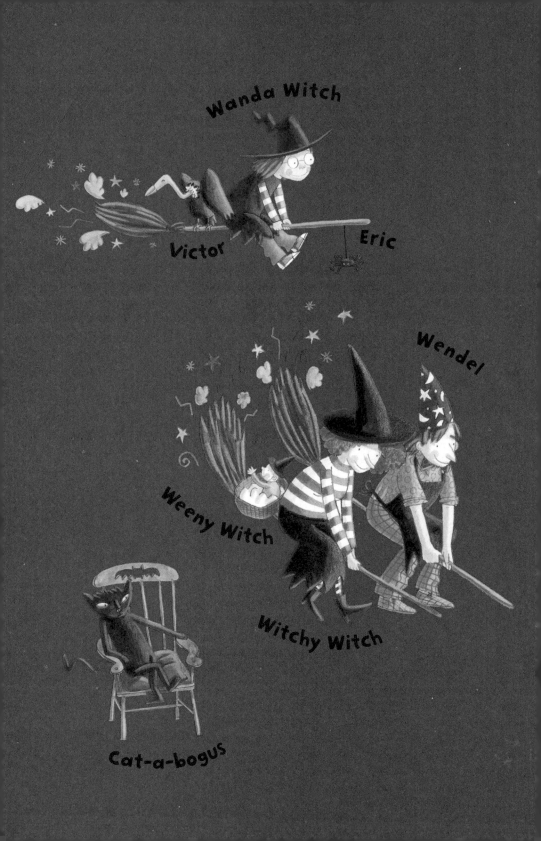

Wanda Witch was always
in trouble with her teacher.
Miss Foulbreath was a real ogre.

It didn't seem fair.
Miss Foulbreath never saw
Primrose looking at herself
in a mirror.

And she never saw Gobby-goblin
poking people with his poky little
finger.

But she *always* saw Wanda Witch
poking him back.

The next time Gobby-goblin poked
her, Wanda Witch put a spell
on him.

The spots didn't
last long.

But Wanda Witch had to write
one hundred times: *I must not do
magic at school.*

Wanda Witch told Cat-a-bogus, "I don't want to go to school anymore."

"Little witches have to go to school," the cat growled, "to learn to read spells."
"I can read," said Wanda Witch.
"Hmmm," purred the cat.
"We'll see about that."

"What does this say?" he asked.
Wanda Witch couldn't read long
words yet, but she tried, anyway.
"Dis-dis…Dizzy Potion?"
she said hopefully.

The cat rolled his eyes.
"I think somebody needs
to do some homework."

"I *can* read," Wanda Witch told Dido. "I could read spells if I wanted to."

Wanda Witch lifted down her
mom's big book of spells.
Just to have a look.

Uh-oh!

Oh, yes! Wanda Witch had always wanted to turn a prince into a frog.

How to Turn a Prince Into a Frog...

fig.1

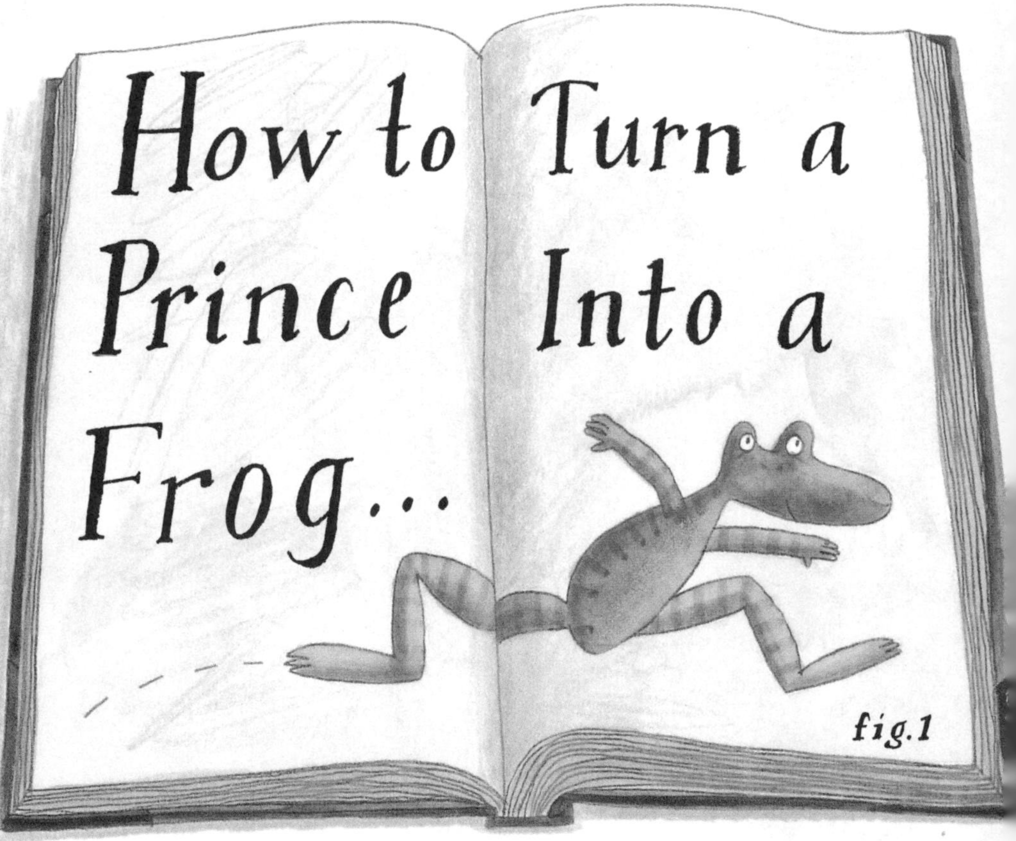

The trouble was she didn't have a
prince right now. "Don't worry,
Victor," said Wanda Witch.
"Spells are easy-breezy."

But this one wasn't.
Wanda Witch didn't
get it all wrong.
Just bits of it.

18

"Turn this vulture into a...frog.
I mean prince!"
There was a *flash*!
And a *crash*!

Wanda Witch was very pleased with herself. The frog wasn't so pleased.

Cro-o-ak!

"Don't worry, Victor," she said, patting his head. "We'll soon have you back."

But then...

...the fat little frog turned into two fat little frogs. Then four, then eight...

In no time at all, the kitchen
was full of frogs!

Wanda Witch tried to sweep them outside.

But the more she swept, the more frogs appeared.

Wanda Witch didn't know what to do next.

The frogs made so much noise,
they woke Cat-a-bogus.

ribbit

The cat didn't like being woken up.

It all went wrong.

"I think someone had better learn to read before she does any more magic," he growled. "Or she could be in *big* trouble!"

With a twitch of his tail and a waggle of his whiskers, the cat did a little magic of his own.

"Up-sy, down-sy, round as well, widdershins-wise, undo this spell."

In a flash, Victor was back.

And all the frogs had disappeared.

Well, almost all of them.

When Mom and Dad came in to say good night, Wanda Witch was reading *The Little Witch's First Book of Spells.*

"How was school today?" they asked.

Wanda Witch smiled.

"I think it will be better tomorrow,"
she said.

How to Turn a
Goblin Into a
Worm ...

Fluency Fun

The words in each list below end in the same sounds.
Read the words in a list.
Read them again.
Read them faster.
Try to read all 15 words in one minute.

better	**little**	**growled**
finger	**people**	**pleased**
never	**simple**	**purred**
teacher	**trouble**	**rolled**
whisker	**waggle**	**turned**

Look for these words in the story.

hundred	**prince**	**magic**
tomorrow	**eight**	